Walking and Walking

Written by Anthony Robinson
Illustrated by Gwyneth Williamson

Collins

We like walking.

3

We like walking in the park.

We like walking on the beach.

We like walking in the woods.

We like walking in the snow.

We like walking home!

Walking

Ideas for reading

Written by Clare Dowdall, PhD
Lecturer and Primary Literacy Consultant

Reading objectives:
- read and understand simple sentences
- use phonic knowledge to decode regular words and read them aloud accurately
- demonstrate understanding when talking with others about what they have read

Communication and language objectives:
- answer "how" and "why" questions about their experiences and in response to stories or events
- listen to stories and respond to what they hear with relevant comments, questions or actions
- develop their own narratives and explanations by connecting ideas or events
- express themselves effectively, showing awareness of listeners' needs

Curriculum links: Physical Development; Knowledge and Understanding of the World

High frequency words: and, we, like, in, the, on

Interest words: walking, park, woods, beach, snow, home

Resources: whiteboard

Word count: 32

Build a context for reading

- Ask children where they like walking and why.

- Look at the front and back covers together. Read the title and describe what is happening in the picture, e.g. *The girl is taking her dog for a walk in the park.*

- Read the blurb together. Practise the high frequency words *we, like, in, the* and the phrase *We like walking.*

Understand and apply reading strategies

- Read pp2–3 together. Point to each word as you read and encourage the children to join in.

- Discuss why the little girl might like walking, e.g. *She likes it because she can play with her dog.*

- Read pp4–5 together. Ask children to make the sound for the phoneme *p* in *park*, and to predict the word using the pictures.

- Ask children to continue to read the book independently and aloud to the end, supporting children as they read, moving around the group and intervening where necessary to praise, encourage and help.